The Kangaroo who couldn't STOP

Robert Cox & Jim Robins

Thomas C. Lothian Pty Ltd
132 Albert Road, South Melbourne, Victoria 3205
www.lothian.com.au

Text copyright © Robert Cox 2004
Illustrations copyright © James Robins 2004

National Library of Australia
Cataloguing-in-Publication data:

Cox, Robert.
  The kangaroo who couldn't stop.

  For children.
  ISBN 0 7344 0658 4.
  ISBN 0 7344 0729 7. (paperback)

  1. Kangaroos - Juvenile fiction. I. Robins, Jim.
  II. Title.

823.92

Designed by Tina Denham
Colour reproduction by Digital Imaging Group, Port Melbourne
Printed in China by SNP Leefung

For Dianna and the children of Hazelbury Bryan School
R.C.

For Tom and Ben
J.R.

Mrs Grey Kangaroo was very worried.
Ever since Keith, her youngest, had found his hop — he couldn't stop!
He'd hopped *all* over Australia.
He'd even hopped up to the top of Uluru and back,
where no other kangaroo had *ever* hopped.

One day Jumper, Thumper and Bumper watched Keith trying to eat his dinner. 'You'll get hop-ups if you're not careful,' said Jumper.

'Hop-ups?' asked Keith. 'What are hop-ups?'

'Hop-ups,' explained Thumper, 'are what you sometimes get if you eat
and drink and hop at the same time.'

'Like this,' said Bumper, and they jerked their shoulders up and down.

'HOP-UP! HOP-UP! HOP-UP! HOP-UP!'

The next day Mrs Grey, Jumper, Thumper, Bumper and Keith went back to see Big Red, the leader of all kangaroos in Australia.

'Good to see you all again,' beamed Big Red, his head going up and down with Keith's hops. 'But please, Keith, can you stop hopping? It's making my neck ache.'

Mrs Grey screwed her lace
handkerchief up into a tiny ball.
'But he … can't!' she burst out.
'Can't?' enquired Big Red.
'Can't what?'
'He can't *stop* hopping now!'
cried Mrs Grey, and ran to Keith,
but caught him mid-hop and could
only hug his back legs.

Big Red was puzzled. 'Does he sleep-hop?' he asked.
'Yes,' replied Mrs Grey. 'Mr Grey is a very light sleeper and gets quite cross with Keith boing-boing-boinging all night long.'

Big Red looked down at Jumper, Thumper
and Bumper.

'Well, in that case,' he said, 'we've got to keep
Keith on the ground long enough to get him used
to NOT hopping. Which means holding on very
tight to his legs.'

So Jumper, Thumper and Bumper caught
Keith's front paws, then his
back legs, and held on tight
until he was quite …

HOPLESS.

Poor Keith felt very uncomfortable because his *outsides* had stopped
hopping but his *insides* couldn't! So he gritted his teeth, clenched his paws,
closed his eyes and went, 'Nnnngggggghhhh!' while Big Red counted,
'One … two … three … four … five … six … seven … eight … nine … ten!'

Jumper, Thumper and Bumper let go and sprang back.
Boing! Up in the air leapt Keith! Boing!

BOING! BOING! BOING! BOING!

And off he hopped in a great big circle.

Big Red shook his big red head and walked over to a nearby cave where
the kangaroos sheltered from the midday sun.

'Now, Jumper, Thumper and Bumper,' he commanded, 'hold on to Keith
again and help him inside the cave. He can't possibly hop in here. The roof
is *much* too low.' So Jumper, Thumper and Bumper giggled and struggled
and gasped and panted until — eventually — they got Keith into the cave.

This time Big Red counted to a hundred.

'One, two, three … fifty-four … seventy-six … ninety-five … ninety-nine …
one hundred!' He peered cautiously inside the cave.

'Well?' whispered Mrs Grey.

'Bunny-hops,' sighed Big Red. 'He's doing little bunny-hops all around the cave. So, we'll try *one* more thing — my *hammock*. He can't *possibly* hop lying on his back.'

Big Red pulled his hammock down very low and said to Keith,
'Jump in! Hop and flop!'

So once again Keith gritted his teeth, clenched his paws, closed his eyes
and went, 'Nnnngghhhh!' Boing!

And landed safely in the middle of the hammock.

But the hammock turned into a trampoline and very soon Keith was
bouncing higher and higher, out of control …
'Good gracious me!' cried Mrs Grey. 'What if he *misses* the hammock?'

Now Big Red, being the leader of all kangaroos in Australia, had his very own billabong next to the trees that held his hammock.

So he waited until Keith was at the bottom of a bounce, then shouted:

'JUMP-INTO-THE-WATER!'

'The only problem is …' said Big Red, as Keith started to fall, 'we haven't had any rain for a long time, and the water isn't very …'

THUD!

'... deep.'

Mrs Grey peered out from behind her handkerchief.

'Is he d… d… d… d…?'

'I'm afraid so,' said Big Red, 'd-ripping with mud. And *still* hopping. And now I've *completely* run out of ideas!'

'Thank heavens,' muttered Mrs Grey to herself, and watched as Big Red took out a large sheet of paper and started to write.

'There you are,' he said, handing the paper to Mrs Grey. 'It's back to the hop-spital to see Dr Leapyear again. If he can cure *hopless* hoppers then I'm sure he can help *non-stop* hoppers.'

So the next day Mrs Grey, Jumper, Thumper and Bumper sat very still in front of Dr Leapyear, the hoptician. Keith hopped on the spot.

The doctor took hold of Keith's front paws and hopped up and down with him for a while, peering into his eyes.

'Hmm,' he said, 'very interesting — *very* interesting indeed,' and he pulled out a watch on a long gold chain, which he began to swing backwards and forwards.

'Hᴏᴘɴᴏsɪs!' declared Dr Leapyear. 'That's the answer! I shall *hopnotise* Keith! But first he must stand *very*, *very* still.'

So Jumper, Thumper and Bumper held very tightly onto Keith's legs once again until only his *insides* were hopping but his *outsides* weren't.

'Splendid!' said Dr Leapyear, and swung the watch in front of Keith's eyes, backwards and forwards, left, right …

Behind Keith the heads of Mrs Grey, Jumper, Thumper and Bumper also went backwards and forwards, left, right, following the watch.

'You're get-ting ve-e-ry slee-ee-py,' said Dr Leapyear in a low, slow, sleepy voice, and then whispered, 'now *close* your eyes … you're getting even *sleepier* …'

BOOMP!

BOOMP!

BOOMP!

BOOMP!

Mrs Grey, Jumper, Thumper and Bumper fell flat on their backs fast asleep — while Keith stood quite still.

'I'm better at this than I thought!' declared Dr Leapyear, and bent down close to Keith.

'Can you hear me?' he whispered softly in Keith's ear.

Keith slowly nodded.

'Then listen *very, very* carefully. When you *want* to hop you will *hop* … and when you want to *stop*, you will *stop*. Do you understand?'

Again Keith nodded slowly.

Dr Leapyear then looked at Mrs Grey to make sure she was fast asleep, and whispered much louder,

'Because if you *don't* …

I'LL DEFINITELY CUT A PIECE OFF YOUR TAIL!'

Keith nodded so fast he almost nodded himself into a hop.

Dr Leapyear clicked his fingers and Keith blinked awake and looked down at his back feet.

They weren't hopping!

Then the doctor woke up Mrs Grey, Jumper, Thumper and Bumper, who rubbed their eyes and to their amazement saw Keith wasn't hopping.

'Has it worked?' gasped Mrs Grey.

Dr Leapyear smiled. 'Hop please, Keith,' he said.

Keith hopped.

'Stop please, Keith.'

Keith stopped.

'HOP, KEITH!

STOP, KEITH!

HOP!

STOP!

HOP!

STOP!

HOP!

STOP!'

Keith bobbed up and down like a yoyo.

Mrs Grey was so overjoyed she ran to Dr Leapyear and hugged him so tight she crushed his watch into little pieces.

'Now children,' said Mrs Grey, 'why don't you all go outside and practise?'

So off they hopped out of the hop-spital — four little kangaroos, hopping for a while, then stopping for a while.

HOPPING AND STOPPING, HOPPING AND STOPPING ...

'What *did* you say to Keith to cure him, Doctor?' asked Mrs Grey, dabbing away a tear with her handkerchief.

'Oh just a little gentle persuasion, my dear,' replied Dr Leapyear. 'Very, very *gentle* persuasion.'

And as he looked up towards the sky, Mrs Grey kissed him.

She really was *very* affectionate.